**Reading
Gems**

I Like
Being Me!

Quarto is the authority on a wide range of topics.

Quarto educates, entertains and enriches the lives of our readers—enthusiasts and lovers of hands-on living.

www.quartoknows.com

First published in 2018 by QED Publishing,
an imprint of The Quarto Group.
The Old Brewery, 6 Blundell Street,
London N7 9BH, United Kingdom.
T (0)20 7700 6700 F (0)20 7700 8066
www.QuartoKnows.com

A catalogue record for this book is available from the British Library.

ISBN 978-1-78493-861-1

Based on the original story by Dreda Blow and Bruno Merz
Author of adapted text: Katie Woolley
Series Editor: Joyce Bentley
Series Designer: Sarah Peden

Manufactured in Dongguan, China TL102017

9 8 7 6 5 4 3 2 1

MIX
Paper from responsible sources
FSC® C104723

This book belongs to

....

Tom liked to dream of being all sorts of things.

One night, he grew flippers and swam in the sea.

"But then," he said, "I like being me."

The next night, Tom dreamt he was a fluffy pink monster.

But the villagers thought he was as cute as could be.

Tom said, "Stop! I want to be me!"

Tom dreamt one night of bubbles and soap.

But it made the floor such a slippery slope.

And stuck in the bath,
Tom wasn't free.

Being made
of water just
isn't for me.

Tom dreamt of a suit of sweets to eat and eat.

But everyone wanted a bite or two or three.

"Stop!" he said. "I want to be me!"

As a spider, Tom met
every sort of bug and flea.

"Yuck," he said.
"I like being me."

At football, he couldn't stop the balls dressed as a tree.

"Sorry," he said. "I play better as me."

When Tom was a flower,
his friends sniffed and sneezed.

"Oh dear," said Tom. "I need to be me."

As a tree, Tom was great for nests, but he couldn't get any rest!

16

And when he dreamt of feathers, he'd try and try but he just couldn't fly into the sky.

A robot boy can't get wet in the rain.

Tom was sad to miss out again.

The rain makes robots too
squeaky, you see.

"I think," he said, "It's time
I was me."

So Tom spent the day in his very own clothes, from his head right down to his toes.

He did a cartwheel,

and danced the jitterbug.

He built a bridge and gave the dog a hug!

Tom ran as fast as he liked. And sang a song with all his might!

But the best bit was hiding where his mum couldn't see.

"Yippee!" he said.

Story Words

bath

bridge

bubbles

bug

clothes

dog

flippers

flower

hide

jitterbug

monster

robot

spider

sweets

tree

Let's Talk About
I Like Being Me!

Look carefully at the front and back cover.

What is Tom doing in the pictures?

How is he feeling?

What things do you like to do on a sunny day?

Tom likes to dream about being different things each night.

Can you remember any of your dreams?

Have ever have had the same dream more than once?

Draw a picture of yourself as a monster.

What would you look like?

Would you be made of fluff or have shiny scales?

What kind of noises might you make?

This story is about learning to like who you are and doing things you enjoy.

Write down three things that you like about yourself.

Write down three activities that you enjoy doing.

What has Tom learned that he likes to do by the end of the story?

Fun and Games

The story has lots of rhyming words.
Can you match up these rhyming pairs?

flea

rest

sky

tree

nest

bug

hug

fly

Complete these story sentences by filling in the gaps with the words below.

robot   bubbles   bug   monster

1. The next night, Tom dreamt he was a fluffy pink _Monster_ .

2. Tom dreamt one night of _~~robot~~ bubbles_ and soap.

3. As a spider, Tom met every sort of .... and flea.

4. A .... boy can't get wet in the rain.

Your Turn

Now that you have read the story,
have a go at telling it in your own words.
Use the pictures below to help you.

5

6

7

8

GET TO KNOW READING GEMS

Reading Gems is a series of books that has been written for children who are learning to read. The books have been created in consultation with a literacy specialist.

The books fit into four levels, with each level getting more challenging as a child's confidence and reading ability grows. The simple text and fun illustrations provide gradual, structured practice of reading. Most importantly, these books are good stories that are fun to read!

Level 1 is for children who are taking their first steps into reading. Story themes and subjects are familiar to young children, and there is lots of repetition to build reading confidence.

Level 2 is for children who have taken their first reading steps and are becoming readers. Story themes are still familiar but sentences are a bit longer, as children begin to tackle more challenging vocabulary.

Level 3 is for children who are developing as readers. Stories and subjects are varied, and more descriptive words are introduced.

Level 4 is for readers who are rapidly growing in reading confidence and independence. There is less repetition on the page, broader themes are explored and plot lines straddle multiple pages.

I like Being Me! uses rhythm and rhyme to tell the story of Tom. It explores themes of dreams, being yourself and body confidence.

Level 3

The next night, Tom dreamt he was a fluffy pink monster.
But the villagers thought he was as cute as could be.

Tom said, "Stop! I want to be me!"

Longer sentences ✓

Wider vocabulary ✓

Varied language ✓

Pictures and words support one another ✓